B144s

School Isn't Fair!

Patricia Baehr

Illustrated by R. W. Alley

FOUR WINDS PRESS   NEW YORK

Printed and bound in Japan

First American Edition   10 9 8 7 6 5 4 3 2 1

The text of this book is set in 14 point Lubalin Graph Book. The illustrations are rendered in pen-and-ink with color pencil and watercolor.

Library of Congress Cataloging-in-Publication Data. Baehr, Patricia Goehner. School isn't fair!/by Patricia Baehr; illustrated by R. W. Alley.—1st American ed.   p.   cm. Summary: Four-year-old Edward describes all the unfair things that happen to him during a school day. ISBN 0-02-708130-3
(1. Fairness—Fiction. 2. Schools—Fiction. 3. Conduct of life—Fiction.) I. Alley, R. W. (Robert W.), ill. II. Title.
PZ7.B1387Sc 1989   (E)—dc19   88-21461 CIP AC

for Peter

and for Jay Munson,
who helps children feel
good about themselves
—P. B.

for Barbara and Manny
—R. W. A.

School isn't fair.

A boy there named
Donny is stronger than
me. That's because he's
five, and I'm only four.
When I get to be five,
he'll be six. When I get
to be six, he'll be seven.
I'll never catch up. That's
not fair.

I try to play with Donny, but he likes to knock me down. He runs and crashes into me and says he is a superhero. I say *I* am a superhero, and he knocks me down again.

So then I say he is a stink head

and lie down very flat on the floor.

During story time, Linda sits on the rug in front of me. She kneels to see the pictures better, but then I can't see them so

I knock *her* down, just like Donny would. Mrs. Monroe stops reading, and I tell her I am a superhero.

She puts me on a chair
in the back of the room
where I can't see the
pictures at all. That's
not fair.

Mrs. Monroe takes out the clay, and I run to put on my smock.

When I get back, all the clay is given out. Wouldn't anyone like to share with Edward? she asks.

Nobody says anything.

They don't even have smocks on.

Mrs. Monroe brings me paints, but I don't want to use them. I just sit and watch the others get clay all over their clothes.

Tamiko makes a clay
heart for me. She calls
it a love.

I want to show her how strong I am, so I growl and
squash the heart with my two hands.

She says I am mean!

Donny and Kenneth and Luke play fireman. They use the rocking boat as a fire engine. I want to ride in it, too, but they say there's no room and I am too little. I tell them I am older than Kenneth, who is playing.

Then Kenneth stands up to show he is bigger. How can that be? Kenneth has new sneakers, just like Luke's. Maybe they make him taller.

For snack we have carrots and apple juice. My
carrot has the stump left on, so I don't eat it.

We get to pour our own juice. I do mine just right, but Linda does hers sloppy and sparkles my shirt. That's not fair.

When we go out to the playground,
Kenneth and Luke get to the glider before
me because they run faster. I think I need
new sneakers. Theirs have pictures of tigers
on them. The only thing on my sneakers
is dirt.

They stay on the glider the whole time, and they
never give me a turn. Not even when I say please.
That's not fair.

If Luke got sick, I could
ride on the glider with
Kenneth.

I tell Luke I hope he
catches a cold.

In music, I get one of the maracas. Donny gets the drum. I like the drum best, but I never get it.

That's not fair.

I want to sing "Jingle
Bells," but everyone says
the time for "Jingle Bells"
is over. I say we can sing
for next year. They sing
"Old MacDonald."

I whisper "Jingle Bells,"
anyway.

When it's time to go
home, Donny can't zip his
jacket.

Since Mrs. Monroe is
helping Linda, I zip
Donny's jacket for him.

He doesn't knock me down.

He says thanks.

Mrs. Monroe tells
everybody that I am the
best at zipping.

I am Super Zipper, I say.
I tell them I can do
buttons, too, and once
I even tied a knot.

In the car, my mother asks
me how school was, and I tell
her what Mrs. Monroe said.
She smiles and says she is
proud of me. I guess I like
being good at zipping.

Maybe I should call
Luke on the phone
when I get home to make
sure he's feeling okay. It wouldn't
be fair if he got sick. He's one of my
best friends.

Tomorrow I think I'll help him zip his jacket.